The Mystery of Moody Manor

by Michelle Dionetti

Wright Group
McGraw-Hill

For Jennifer, who shows the way,
and for Christian, the garden wizard,
and for Ernest, the center of the maze

The Mystery of Moody Manor
Text copyright © Michelle Dionetti
Illustrations copyright © Wright Group/McGraw-Hill
Illustrations by Taylor Bruce

Ragged Island Mysteries™ is a trademark of The McGraw-Hill
Companies, Inc.

Wright Group/McGraw-Hill
19201 120th Avenue NE, Suite 100
Bothell, WA 98011
www.WrightGroup.com

Printed in the United States of America

10 9 8 7 6 5 4 3

ISBN: 0-322-01591-X
ISBN: 0-322-01655-X (6-pack)

Jinx

Allie

Liz

Drew

Puffin

CONTENTS

1

THE MYSTERIOUS STRANGERS

Jinx Harris was going to crash.

The front of the Moody mansion came right at him. Rows of windows three stories high and yellow walls rushed closer. Jinx tried to brake. But his cousin Liz's old bike was too big for him. One more moment and Jinx Harris would be house paint.

Part of the drive curved around the mansion. Jinx steered onto that. He took the curve too fast. He couldn't stop.

Jinx steered into a bush. It was a big bush. In a month or two it would be covered with pink flowers.

"Don't hurt me," begged Jinx.

THWACK!

Branches shook. It sounded worse than it felt. But Jinx didn't move right away. He felt like every window in the big house was a face, laughing at him. This would be a good place for ghosts, if he believed in ghosts.

Jinx backed Liz's bike away from the bush. He hoped he hadn't broken any branches. Lester Moody had hired him to clean up the loose brush on the Moody estate, not to make more. Lester said he'd meet Jinx here after school Friday. That was now. Part of Jinx was glad his new boss wasn't here yet. The rest of him wished Lester would hurry up.

The Moody mansion stood on the east side of Ragged Island. The house and its grounds were so big the islanders called the place Moody Manor. The mansion had twenty-three rooms inside and the Atlantic Ocean for a side yard. Jinx wasn't thrilled to be here alone. An army could camp behind the house, and he'd never know they were there.

Jinx looked at the bush he had used for a landing pad.

"Thanks," Jinx told it. "You saved my

life." He wouldn't be surprised if the bush talked back. Moody Manor was like that.

"Talking to trees, now?"

Jinx jumped a foot. Was he glad to see his good friend Drew Ellis! Drew was big, and he was calm except when he thought something wasn't fair.

"Hi, bud!" said Jinx. "I didn't hear you bike up!"

"Mom agreed to let me work with you today," said Drew. "What are you doing?"

"I crashed into this bush," said Jinx. He wouldn't admit it to anyone but Drew. "This is Liz's old bike. I'm not used to it yet."

"What happened to YOUR bike?" Drew asked.

Jinx could not wait to answer that question. He stuck out his chest. "MY bike," he said, "is too SMALL."

Jinx was the shortest kid in Ragged

Island's sixth grade. For him, growing was better than a good report card.

"No kidding!" said Drew.

"That's why I'm working here!" said Jinx. "I need money for a new bike."

"Looks like there's plenty of work," said Drew.

The grounds went on and on. There were stables and a woodshed back here. Gardens stretched far behind the house.

"Does Moody Manor belong to Lester Moody?" asked Drew.

"No, to his older brother Earl," said Jinx. "But no one knows where Earl is. Gramp says he has been missing for thirty years."

Jinx's Gramp knew stories about everyone from Ragged Island.

"Maybe Earl is dead," said Drew.

Jinx shivered. Maybe that's who was watching from inside the house when he crashed! Earl Moody's ghost!

"Gramp says no one knows who owns Moody Manor now," said Jinx. "He says that half the Moodys on Ragged Island want to claim a piece of it."

Most island Moodys were somehow related to Arthur Moody, the first white settler of Ragged Island. Arthur's grandson Henry had built Moody Manor 150 years ago. Henry Moody had one son, William, and two grandsons. His grandsons were Earl and Lester. Now Lester Moody was the only one left of the Henry Moody family.

"Maybe Brett Moody is one of the Moodys who wants the manor," said Drew. "I saw him on my way here."

"No kidding?" said Jinx.

Brett was related to the Moodys who lived on the mainland, not to Henry Moody.

"Lester says someone broke into the

house over the winter," said Jinx.

"I hope it wasn't Brett," said Drew. "I feel sort of sorry for him. His dad's always mad about something."

Jinx nodded. Brett had a temper, and sometimes his teasing turned mean. But Jinx felt kind of sorry for him too.

"Whoever broke into the house didn't take anything," said Jinx. "Just moved stuff around."

"That does sound like kids," said Drew.

"Or Earl Moody's ghost," joked Jinx. At least he hoped he was joking.

Lester Moody drove his old truck up to the stables. Lester was bony and lean, with thick gray hair. Except for the gray, you couldn't guess his age.

"This is Drew Ellis," said Jinx. "He can work with me today, if it's okay."

Lester looked at Drew and nodded. "Got

enough work for two," he said.

"Where do we start, Mr. Moody?" asked Drew.

"Call me Lester," said Lester.

Lester strode to what used to be the stables. He unlocked the end one. Once there were horses inside. Now there were tools. Lester got out wheelbarrows, clippers, and rakes. Then he led the boys to the front of the house.

Jinx was glad the sun was out. The day before had been stormy, with a strong wind blowing off the ocean. The sun had glinted on little whitecaps, and the waves were noisy.

"I want you to clean up the shrubs in front of the house," said Lester. "Some people rented the place for the weekend. They said Moody Manor was just what they were looking for. They might rent it for

the whole summer."

Jinx thought he would like Moody Manor better with people inside. He watched as Lester showed them where he wanted them to clip, where to rake, and where to dump the brush.

"Tomorrow I'll work here with you," said Lester. "Today I have to finish the library grounds. I'll be back by five. Don't leave till I get here. I want to lock the tools away. If I don't, they'll get stolen. It's happened before."

Jinx looked at Drew. Did ghosts use tools? Did Brett Moody? Maybe he and Drew could find out who was messing with Moody Manor!

Lester left. Jinx raked till he thought his arms would fall off. How many leaves could fit under one bush anyway? His rake struck something hard—a metal hinge.

"I wonder what this is doing here?" he said.

"Let me see," said Drew.

Jinx handed him the hinge.

"It looks old," said Drew.

"Yeah," agreed Jinx. The hinge was big and black and made of iron.

He and Drew looked at the front of Moody Manor. The window shutters had

10

hinges, but the ones on the
nearby windows were all
where they belonged.

Jinx slid behind the
bushes. He took a good
look at the nearest window.
Locked tight! No one had gotten in this
way! Jinx peered through the window. They
could hold a town meeting in the room
inside! What family could use so many chairs
and sofas?

"There's no hinge missing here either,"
said Drew from the next window.

"Let's dump the brush," said Jinx, "and
check the hinges on the stable doors!"

They had to dump the brush behind the
stables. Jinx emptied his wheelbarrow. He
started back around the stable.

"This has to be it!" said a man's voice.

11

Jinx froze. What a strange voice! It was soft, with a drawl.

"You say that every time," said a man with a deeper voice.

"This is the one," insisted the first man. "I can feel it in my bones. We're so close I can taste it!"

2
PUZZLES

Jinx pushed Drew back into the shadows.

"I saw two guys out there!" he whispered.

"Huh?" said Drew.

"Cowboys!" he hissed.

At least the men looked like his idea of cowboys. They wore cowboy boots and big hats. Jinx peered around the edge of the stables. He watched the younger man pull his hat low over his face. The man had thick, blond hair that almost reached his shoulders. Huge sunglasses hid his eyes.

"This has got to be it, Clay," said the other man, the one with the soft voice. He had a friendly face and thick eyebrows. "Three floors! A gazebo!"

A gazebo? What was a gazebo?

"Right on the ocean!" said the man.

"That doesn't mean this is the RIGHT place," said Clay. "Or even that there really IS a place. You're nuts to believe her anyhow. She was confused before she died, Roy."

"There IS a place," said the older man— Roy. "Just like she said. Somewhere on the shore of a Maine island."

Both men got quiet. Jinx could tell they were mad at each other. He guessed this was an old fight.

"We'd best get back to the ferry landing,"

said Roy. "We'll get groceries at that general store and meet the boys. They said they'd take the five o'clock ferry, after the movie on the mainland gets out. I hope they like this place. I hope we've finally found what we're looking for."

"This is the third try, Roy," said Clay. "Give it up. We can't island-hop forever. Maine is a long way from Texas."

"I'm not giving up," said Roy. "I'm doing

this for my boys, Clay. And for you, bro. I'm doing this for you, too."

Jinx watched Clay look around. Clay's head turned slowly. His sunglasses looked like a lighthouse beacon.

"At least we'll be out of the way here," said Clay. "With luck I won't have to see anyone for weeks. Just you and the boys."

Jinx pulled his head back and held his breath. Out of the way? Maybe that Clay guy was in hiding!

Jinx tried to hear more, but the men had stopped talking. After what seemed like forever, he risked another peek.

"They're gone!" he said.

Drew ran out and stared toward the road. "There goes a car!" he cried.

Jinx saw a white car turn onto the road.

"Those must be the guys renting Moody Manor," said Jinx. "What do you think they meant? About the 'right place'?"

"Beats me," said Drew. "But they said a place with three floors."

"Yeah," said Jinx. "And a gaz...gaz—"

"Gazebo," finished Drew. He pointed to the gardens. "I think that white thing is a gazebo," he said.

Jinx looked. The white thing was a kind of freestanding porch. It had a peaked roof and six sides. Why would the Texans be looking for that?

"I bet those guys know about old smugglers' treasure or something!" said Jinx. "Maybe they have a map, and they're looking for the place the map is about!"

"You wish!" said Drew.

"But that guy said, 'We're so close I can taste it!'" said Jinx. "He's looking for something!"

"We should get back to work," said Drew.

17

Jinx grabbed his wheelbarrow. "Let's finish raking," he said. "I want to look at that gazebo before Lester comes back!"

"The hinge," reminded Drew.

"Oh, yeah!"

Jinx and Drew checked the stable doors. One of them had a missing hinge.

"That's how someone got to the tools," said Jinx. "Maybe they wanted tools so they could break into the house."

"Hey!" said Drew. "Maybe the Texans and whoever is breaking into Moody Manor want to find the same thing!"

Jinx's heart skipped a beat. "Maybe we can find whatever it is first!"

They headed back to the front of the house.

"I wish I could work HERE tomorrow," said Drew.

Drew had to work at his dad's place most

Saturdays—Mel's Diner. Jinx knew he hated the noise and rush and grease. Drew liked fresh air and quiet.

"Sleep over at my house tomorrow night," said Jinx. "I'll fill you in!"

They got back to work. Jinx wished he had a radio. Instead he listened to the island music of ocean washing the rocks offshore, seagulls, a slamming door...

A slamming door?

"Did you hear that?" he asked Drew. "That sound?" His neck prickled. Was someone breaking into Moody Manor right now?

"Naw," said Drew. "It's nothing."

Jinx wasn't sure. Maybe it WAS nothing. Maybe nothing ALIVE.

"Hey you guys!" called a voice.

Two runners came down Moody Manor's long drive. One was Jinx's cousin Liz French.

The other was their friend and classmate Allie Davies.

"Liz went to Allie's after school," Jinx told Drew. "I told her we'd be here."

Liz reached them first. She lifted her hair off her shoulders and puffed. Liz ran everywhere. She was fast. Allie could almost keep up with her. Allie had long legs, short black hair, and lots of energy.

"This place is great!" said Allie. "Show us around!"

"Help us first," said Jinx. "You'll like it! Raking is fun!"

"No way, Tom Sawyer!" said Liz.

Liz knew Jinx too well. She lived right next door to him on Rocky Point. She'd always lived next door to him. Their mothers were sisters.

"But listen!" said Jinx.

He and Drew told Liz and Allie about someone breaking into Moody Manor. They told them about the missing tools, the Texans, and what the men had said.

"It does sound like the men are looking for something particular," said Liz.

"Like a hideout," said Allie. "The RIGHT hideout!"

"The one where the money is hidden," said Jinx.

"Money is all you think about!" said Liz. "Maybe they aren't looking for money! Maybe they want the answer to a puzzle."

"Or maybe they're looking for something they don't want anyone else to find," said Allie.

"Maybe if they find what they're looking for, they won't have to be in hiding anymore," said Drew.

"Yeah," said Jinx "Like loot from a bank robbery. Like smugglers' treasure."

Jinx looked at the bushes left to clip. He just HAD to check out that gazebo before Lester came back! "Help us out, Liz," he pleaded. "Didn't I help you wax the floors last week?"

Liz's mom—Jinx's Aunt Jean—ran the Rocky Point Bed and Breakfast. They waxed the place's wood floors twice a year, spring and fall. Somehow Liz always ended up waxing. And somehow Liz's sixteen-year-old sister, The Beautiful Marla, always got out of it.

"Okay, okay," said Liz. "Let's get it over with."

Jinx grinned at her. Liz was all right. They set to work.

"What's this?" asked Liz. She bent over, then held up a baseball cap.

"Bellport Pirates," read Jinx.

Bellport was the town on the mainland coast. A ferry ran back and forth between Ragged Island and Bellport.

"Who do we know on the Bellport Pirates?" asked Drew.

The Pirates were the Bellport High School baseball team. Up until the eighth grade, Ragged Island kids went to school on the island. For high school, they ferried over to the mainland every day.

23

"I'll bet it's Brett Moody," said Jinx. "Or some other Moody. Maybe they come out here to dream about owning the place."

"Maybe we can find out whose cap this is," said Allie. "It looks new, like someone lost it this year. It would be a whole other color if it had been out here all winter."

"I'll keep it with the hinge," said Jinx.

He showed Allie and Liz the hinge he had found. Maybe the cap and the hinge added up to something.

The chance of finding more clues made raking more interesting. With four of them working, the friends soon finished cleaning up the front of the house.

"Looks good!" said Allie.

"Let's go see that gazebo!" said Jinx.

They brought their tools back to the stables.

"Hey!" said Drew. "Do you see what I see?"

24

He pointed up. Jinx looked up at the slanted roof on the second floor of the manor's wing. The roof butted into the side of the mansion. On the third floor, near the roof, a window stood open.

Wide enough to let a person in. Or a ghost out.

3

HIDING PLACES

"Do you think someone's up there right now?" asked Liz.

"How could they get by without us seeing them?" asked Drew.

"From the back," said Allie. "Anyone could come through the woods! The house is so huge we'd never notice!"

"Did you two see anyone on your way here?" asked Jinx.

"Just Beth Pinsky," said Liz, "in her new truck."

Beth Pinsky was a carpenter. She restored old houses. Jinx bet they were the kind with old iron hinges on the doors and shutters.

"Where was she?" asked Drew.

"Just past the turnoff to Moody Manor," said Liz. "Why? Did you see her?"

"No," said Drew.

"But maybe we heard her," said Jinx. He thought of the sound of the door slamming. Had it been a truck door? Or was it the sound of someone landing on the roof? Or pulling open a window?

"No one's been here since we got here," said Allie. "Have they?"

They all looked at each other.

"No one has been in the FRONT of the house, anyway," said Liz.

"Maybe it was open all along," said Allie.

Jinx tried to think back. When he crashed

into the bush and thought someone was watching, maybe someone was!

"I still want to check out the gazebo," said Jinx. "But we'd better bring the tools with us. Just in case."

They took the rakes, clippers, and wheelbarrows to the gardens with them.

"These grounds look like a movie set!" said Liz in a hushed voice.

They looked like a lot of yard work to Jinx. There were acres of lawn, with fancy flower beds cut into the grass. Next came the gazebo; then a wall of high hedges.

"That must be the famous Puzzle Hedge," said Allie.

Jinx had heard about the Puzzle Hedge. It was all high bushes and paths that formed a maze. When you walked through, you could get lost. Jinx didn't even want to think about having to clean up the Puzzle Hedge.

29

But what a great place to hide something! Or to hide out!

Liz reached the gazebo first. She bounded up the steps.

"Good view!" she reported.

Jinx had to agree when he saw the wide open ocean, a lobster boat, and Moody Manor from the back. He looked up at the gazebo's rafters. There were plenty of hiding places up there. No treasure maps, though, or bags of jewels.

"If the gazebo makes this the RIGHT place," said Jinx, "what do you think the Texans are looking for?"

"It doesn't have to be a THING," said Liz. "Maybe they're looking for the place their grandparents got married."

"No way!" said Jinx.

He knew where that idea came from. Liz's parents had just gotten divorced. Marriage and divorce were pretty much all Liz thought about these days.

"Maybe they knew someone who visited the place they're looking for a long time

31

ago," argued Liz. "Maybe that person left something important there."

"Sure!" said Jinx. "Like loot from a bank robbery! And maybe THAT would explain why Clay wants an out-of-the-way place! Maybe his face is on a *WANTED* poster because of the bank robbery, and the money from the robbery is missing!"

"That doesn't make any sense," said Allie. "If Clay robbed a bank, wouldn't he know where the money was?"

"Not if his partner hid it!" said Jinx.

"What partner?" asked Drew.

"The partner that hid the money in a house on a Maine island!" said Jinx.

"You have a one-track mind!" said Liz.

Hey, that wasn't fair! So did she! Enough talk. Jinx wanted to find the gazebo's secret. He went back down to the grass. Criss-cross wood trim went all around the gazebo. Jinx peered through the lattice into the space underneath the gazebo.

"Guys, come look at this!" he called.

Drew, Liz, and Allie came to see.

"Garbage!" said Liz.

Jinx found a hinged place in the lattice. He pulled it open and crawled under the gazebo. Allie came in right behind him. They poked through the garbage.

"Candy wrapper," said Allie.

"Pen," said Jinx. "The kind everyone uses." He held it up.

"Looks like snack and homework time at my house," said Allie.

Allie lived in a full house. She was the oldest of five kids.

"We'd better tell Lester about this," said Drew. "Someone's been hanging out here."

"Lester!" said Jinx. "What time is it? Do we have time for the Puzzle Hedge?"

Drew looked at his watch. "Quarter to five," he said. "We'd better go back."

"You go," said Allie. "It's low tide. I want to check out Urchin Cave. Are you coming, Liz?"

Urchin Cave was set into the rocks on the Moody Manor shoreline. At high tide the cave was covered by ocean. At low tide you could climb into the cave if you were careful. The rocks in front of it were underwater half the time, so they were covered with slippery seaweed. And barnacles. The rocks inside the cave were covered with seaweed, too, and mussels and sea urchins. The sea urchins looked like little spiny pincushions. They were beautiful colors—blue, purple, and pink. Urchin Cave was magical. But you had to watch out. If the tide came up while you were inside, the cave filled with water. You would drown.

Jinx watched the girls disappear over the rocks. Did Urchin Cave have treasure? Like pirate gold?

Like whatever the Texans were after?

4

THE MOODY MANOR STORY

Jinx steered Liz's old bike down the dirt road to Rocky Point. It was a two-house road. First came the Rocky Point Bed and Breakfast—one large house and five cabins. Liz lived there with her mother and The Beautiful Marla. Off to the side was the little house Jinx shared with his mom and dad.

Jinx was starving. He banged in the back door of his house. Bad news—no dinner smells!

"Hi, Mom!" he shouted. "Aren't we eating?"

His dog, Chief, jumped up to lick him hello. Chief was half German shepherd, half Lab, big and friendly.

Then his mom burst into the kitchen. She was short and quick, with dark, curly hair. "We're eating at the B and B," she said. "Let's go. Dad's already over there. Gramp too."

"I can't make it that far," groaned Jinx. Even Chief's dog food looked good. He grabbed an apple to keep from fainting.

Chief won the race to the bed and breakfast. The big kitchen smelled great.

"Chili, I hope?" asked Jinx. Aunt Jean made great chili.

"Yup," said Dad.

He stood at the stove, stirring the chili. Dad was on the short side like Jinx, and stocky. Unlike Jinx, he could fix anything.

"When do we eat?" asked Jinx.

"Five minutes," said Aunt Jean.

She had Liz's wiry brown hair. She used to have Liz's sense of humor too, before the divorce.

"I can't wait five minutes!" said Jinx.

"You always were hungrier than a moose in winter, James Xavier," said Gramp.

James Xavier was Jinx's real name.

"Gramp!" he said. "I want to ask you about Moody Manor!"

"That so?" said Gramp. "What for?"

"Because I started working for Lester Moody this week," said Jinx.

"Up to Moody Manor?" asked Gramp.

Jinx nodded. "You know the story about Earl Moody?"

"Yup," said Gramp. "It begins back about thirty years ago. William Moody, Lester and Earl's dad, wanted Earl to become a lawyer.

39

Young Earl wanted to see the world. He got on a merchant ship to Russia. Went to Greece, too, as I remember it. Ended up in Texas."

"Texas!" said Jinx.

"What happened to him?" asked Liz.

"No one knows," said Gramp. "The family only heard from Earl now and then. Maybe Earl was still mad at his father about law school. Or maybe he just hated to write letters. Last anyone heard from him, he was in Texas. There was some talk he had been fishing for shrimp on the Gulf."

"Is he dead?" asked Liz.

"That's the guess," said Gramp. Earl and Lester's ma, Thelma, wanted to hire a detective to track Earl down. William was still mad at Earl. He wouldn't hear of it."

"How come no one lives at Moody Manor now?" asked Liz.

"House came to Earl in his father's will," said Gramp. "Lester got a heap of land; Earl got the house. There's a number of Moodys after the place now. They took the matter to court. It'll take the lawyers years to settle."

The back door opened. The Beautiful

41

Marla came in, followed by Jinx's big brother, Mike. Mike was twenty-one now. He lived in his own place in Bellport.

"Mike!" said everybody.

"Hi, folks!" said Mike. "I ran into Marla in Bellport and decided to come to the island for dinner!"

Jinx knew he and Mike looked a lot alike. Same round face and blue eyes. Mike was on the short side too, for a man.

"You should see who I met on the ferry!" said The Beautiful Marla. She tilted her head, and her honey-blond hair swirled. "Two boys from out west! They had on those hats, you know? Like in a western movie? The older one was really handsome!"

Jinx and Liz looked at one another.

"How old were they?" asked Jinx.

"The older one is the perfect age for me!" said Marla. "The other one's more your age—perfect for Liz!"

"Get out!" said Liz.

She hated The Beautiful Marla's boy talk.

Jinx was pretty sure Liz wouldn't turn into The Beautiful Elizabeth when she was sixteen, but he intended to keep an eye on her, just in case.

"Anyone with them?" asked Jinx.

"Two men met them at the ferry landing when we got off," said Mike.

"The men had hats too," said Marla. "One of them was dressed all in black and wore sunglasses. He looked like an outlaw!"

"Those are the guys," Jinx told Liz.

"What guys?" asked Marla.

"The ones who rented Moody Manor for the weekend," said Jinx.

"Really?" squealed Marla. "Where you're working?"

"Yup," said Jinx.

"I'm going with you tomorrow!" said Marla.

"No, you're not," said Jinx.

But The Beautiful Marla had that look in her eye—the one that said she was going to do what she wanted.

"Give it up, Jinx," said Liz.

Jinx groaned.

Aunt Jean distracted them with food. Jinx had never tasted anything as good as fresh-baked bread dunked into Aunt Jean's chili. Maybe it was the food, but finally Jinx's brain began to work.

The last anyone had heard of Earl Moody, he had been in Texas. Were the Texans who rented Moody Manor looking to find something Earl had told them about?

But wait—if they knew about Earl Moody and Moody Manor, they'd know Moody Manor was the place they wanted. They could have found it first try. So what they were looking for must have nothing to do with Earl Moody.

Unless—what if the Texans had never heard of Earl Moody? But they'd heard something he said about treasure? After all, Texas was the last place anyone saw Earl before he disappeared.

After dinner, Jinx and Mike took Chief for a walk. Stars lit up the grass between the Harris house and the bed and breakfast. They lit up a truck on the driveway too.

Chief took off, barking.

"Who's there?" called Mike.

"Beth Pinsky."

Beth Pinsky! "Chief, come!" called Jinx.

Chief didn't come. But he stopped barking. Jinx caught up with him and grabbed his collar. He could see Beth now, standing in the light from the porch light. Jinx wanted to like her, but he didn't think she had a sense of humor. He'd never seen her smile.

"I'm looking for your cousin Liz," said Beth. "Didn't I see her at Moody Manor today?"

"She was there," said Jinx. "So was I."

"You were?" said Beth. "Then maybe you

46

found something I lost."

"What?" asked Jinx. A baseball cap?

"A hammer," said Beth.

"Haven't seen it," said Jinx.

But his mind raced. Someone besides Lester was missing tools! Or was Beth's story a bluff? Maybe she was the one who had taken Lester's tools. Maybe she came asking questions because she knew Liz had seen her near Moody Manor!

"Why would your tools be at Moody Manor?" asked Mike.

"I restore old houses," said Beth. "I worked there with Lester last winter."

"Oh," said Jinx. That explained that. "I'll keep my eyes open tomorrow," he said.

"Okay, thanks," mumbled Beth.

She got into her truck and drove away.

"Now that was weird," said Mike. "If she missed a tool from last winter, why would she ask about it now?"

"Maybe she just found out it's missing," said Jinx.

"Still weird," said Mike. "Why not just ask Lester about it?"

"There have been break-ins," said Jinx. "Today we found an open window. Lester said HE didn't open it!"

"Weirder and weirder," said Mike.

They sat on the front steps while Chief ran around.

"You ever been out to Moody Manor?" Jinx asked Mike.

"Sure," said Mike. "I used to take Marla and her friends out there when she was little." Mike grinned, a grin like Jinx's. "I got them lost in the Puzzle Hedge. And I made them think Moody Manor was haunted."

Jinx wished he'd thought of it! "How did you do that?" he asked.

"I blew up a balloon, then let the air squeal out of it," said Mike. "I told them it was a ghost caught in a broken window."

"What else?" asked Jinx.

"I rolled a marble across the gazebo floor," said Mike. "I told them it was a trap door, sliding open to swallow them up."

Jinx laughed. Then he told Mike about the Texans and what he'd heard them say.

"Maybe they're looking for a place to shoot a movie," said Mike.

Jinx stared at his brother. "Yeah!" he said. "Why didn't I think of that?"

"Because your mind is always on buried treasure," said Mike.

"Moody Manor would make a great setting! Maybe I could be an extra!" said Jinx. Did they pay extras?

"You'd better just do your job," said Mike, "and not bug the tourists."

"Yeah, yeah," said Jinx.

He had a lot to do tomorrow. He had to find out what the Texans were really looking for and why Beth Pinsky had really come to Rocky Point. He fell asleep thinking about ghost stories, though, and how he would haunt The Beautiful Marla if he had the chance.

5

MARLA ON THE MOVE

Saturday was a great workday, sunny and still. When Jinx got outside his house, he saw three girls on the front porch of the B and B—Liz, Marla, and Delia Clark. Delia Clark was in the third grade. She had bright red hair and bright blue eyes. And she thought The Beautiful Marla was some kind of princess. She'd been hanging around Marla a lot lately.

"Jinx!" cried Marla. "I'm coming too!"

"No way!" Jinx called back. He got on Liz's bike.

"Can I come?" Delia asked.

"Liz!" said Jinx.

"Forget it," said Liz. "The Beautiful Marla has made up her mind."

"Wait," said Marla. "I forgot my hairbrush."

She went in after it. Delia went in too.

"Now's your chance," said Liz.

Jinx sped off. He didn't care if he had to crash-land. He wanted to get to Moody Manor before Marla did. When he turned onto Rim Road, he saw another bicycle rider. The cyclist wheeled out of the turnoff for Moody Manor. Brett Moody?

Jinx tore after him.

"Brett!" he shouted.

The boy turned around. His eyes looked like daggers.

"Wait up!" called Jinx. He pedaled Liz's bike like mad. He hoped he could stop it without making a fool of himself.

"Did you lose a cap?" called Jinx. "A Bellport Pirates cap?"

"Maybe," said Brett. "Why?"

Jinx caught up to Brett, then slowed down carefully. "I found a cap," said Jinx. "In

the bushes outside Moody Manor."

He tried to sound normal. Like he didn't mean Brett was a snoop. Or maybe a thief. He watched Brett try to decide whether to claim the cap.

"Not mine," said Brett.

Was that a lie? Jinx couldn't tell. He biked on to Moody Manor and coasted to a stop at the front door. He had to tilt the bike and hop on one foot to keep from falling.

The man named Roy opened the door. "Howdy," he said.

"Hi," said Jinx. "I'm Jinx Harris. I do yard work here."

"A hardworking Yankee boy! Well, son, my name is Roy True. I'm mighty pleased to meet you," said Roy. "Y'all sure have a beautiful island here."

"Thanks," said Jinx.

"Tell me," said Roy. "Do you know of any

ship merchants who used to live on your island?"

Jinx's heart skipped. Ship merchants! Maybe Roy wanted to find lost cargo! "Henry Moody was a ship merchant," he said. "He built this place."

"Do tell!" Roy exclaimed.

Roy gazed back into the mansion, a secret smile on his face. Jinx wanted to ask about cargo. But Roy spoke first.

"My boys will want to meet you," he said.

He put his fingers to his mouth and gave a shrill whistle. Two boys appeared.

Jinx gave them a good look. The one his age had dark, thick eyebrows and watching eyes. The older one had curly dark hair and a wide mouth. HE was Marla's heartthrob.

"Boys," said Roy, "this here is a son of the

island, Jinx Harris. Jinx, this is Lee."
Roy put a hand on the younger boy's
shoulder. "And that one's Sonny."

"Hi," said Jinx.

Lee stepped outside. "You live here?" he
asked. "All year long?"

"All year long and all my life," said Jinx.
"Where are you from?"

"Lubbock, Texas," said Lee.

"Been to Maine before?" asked Jinx.

"Yes," said Lee. "Cranberry Island. Swans
Island. We're look—"

Roy poked him in the back.

"We like Maine," finished Lee.

Lester came around the house.

"Jinx," he said. "Get some logs from the
woodpile and bring them in. We need some
in the living room fireplace. And up in the
bedrooms."

"I'll help," said Lee.

Jinx showed Lee where the woodshed was. They each grabbed some logs.

"What are you going to do while you're here?" asked Jinx.

"Explore every inch of the place," said Lee. "Inside and out."

"Looking for what?" asked Jinx.

Lee opened his mouth, then closed it.

Rats! Jinx tried again. "How come you keep coming to Maine islands?" he asked.

"We started coming to Maine when my mother died, three years ago," said Lee. "Pa always wanted to explore the Maine islands. He says we'll try a new island each time till we find the right one."

The right one for what? But they'd reached the house. Jinx followed Lee inside. Portraits of dead Moodys hung all over the place. They were old oil paintings, and they were all dark. Everyone in them looked stern, like life at Moody Manor was no picnic.

From the hall, Jinx saw three rooms you could call living rooms. He stepped into the smallest one. It was still as big as his whole downstairs.

"Let's put the logs in here," he said. "This room will be easiest to heat."

They went out for more wood.

"How can your father spend all summer in Maine?" Jinx asked Lee. "Doesn't he have to work?"

Lee's bushy eyebrows drew together. "He flies back and forth," he said. "Uncle Clay stays with us."

Jinx wondered what kind of work that could be. Movie work? Or bank robbery?

"You go to school on the island?' asked Lee.

Jinx talked about Ragged Island School.

He told Lee how the sixth grade had thirteen kids in it, total. When they got back to the house, they ran into The Beautiful Marla.

"I saw that girl on the boat yesterday," said Lee. "What's she doing here?"

"Jinx!" said Marla. "Hi! I'll help you get wood!"

Lee looked at Jinx.

"She's my cousin," Jinx had to say. "We've got it, Marla," he told her.

"Then I'll get kindling!" said Marla.

She ran off. Her honey-blond hair bounced.

"I guess there's no stopping her," said Lee.

"You got that right," said Jinx.

Inside, Lee led Jinx up the long staircase. They walked past more portraits.

"There are eight bedrooms up here," said Lee. "Just on this floor!"

They took wood to two rooms.

"We need one more load of wood," said Lee. "But I'll get it."

Jinx nodded. He went downstairs. Marla passed him with a load of sticks and twigs. Clay and Roy stood at the foot of the stairs. No—that was Clay and Lester. Clay had his sunglasses on—in the house.

The men looked up.

"Your grandpa still lobstering?" asked Lester.

"He keeps a few traps," said Jinx.

"Clay here wants some lobster," said Lester. "Think you can get some for us?"

"I'll call and see," said Jinx.

"Phone's in the kitchen," said Lester.

Jinx found the kitchen in the wing that had been added onto the house. It had a worn wood floor and a big metal sink. The walls were a horrible green, like pea soup.

60

Jinx called Gramp. Liz answered.

"What are you doing there?" asked Jinx.

"Allie's doing a paper," said Liz. "It's on the history of lobstering on the island. She's talking to Gramp. Delia and I came too."

"Let me talk to Gramp," said Jinx.

Gramp got on the line. Jinx explained what he wanted.

"I hauled up five lobsters today," said Gramp. "Liz can take them over."

Jinx reported back to Lester.

"Good," said Lester. "Let's get to that brush."

Clay stared at Jinx. Yikes. With the sunglasses and the black hat, Clay looked like an evil robot from Texas.

61

"We'll stay out of your way," said Jinx.

"That will be good," said Clay.

It sounded like a threat. Maybe Jinx should forget about trying to find out why the Texans were there. Maybe it was too dangerous to pry!

6
SWEPT AWAY!

Sonny came down the stairs at a fast clip and bolted out the door. Jinx hid a grin. He must have run into The Beautiful Marla up there.

Lester took Jinx outside. They drove the truck down to the end of the driveway.

"We'll clean the brush out along here," said Lester.

Rats. How could Jinx find anything out so far away from the house?

Lester wasn't the talking type. He worked

hard, and Jinx had to work hard too, to keep up. While he worked, he kept an eye on Lee and Sonny. They went into the stables, then the gardens. The house hid them from view. What were they doing? Jinx would give anything to follow them! Instead he pulled garbage out of the leaves—a paper cup, an old newspaper, and a cloth glove. People were pigs.

"Where does all this stuff come from?" he asked Lester.

"Moody Manor's fan club," said Lester. "The ones who hope Moody Manor will be theirs someday."

He sounded mad enough to spit nails.

Jinx remembered Beth Pinsky. He told Lester about the hammer. Lester scowled.

"Hammers, hinges, open windows!" he said. "Yesterday, after you told me about the mess under the gazebo, I looked for more signs of trespassers. I found a broken window latch on the first floor! It wouldn't surprise me if they found a way to crawl through that window!"

He pulled a branch out of the brush and snapped it in two. Jinx felt bad for Lester. What would it be like not to see your brother for thirty years? And what if people broke into your house because they wanted it for themselves?

"I'm going to get an ax," said Lester.

He strode away. Jinx picked up a pile of brush to throw into the truck bed. Underneath was a coiled rope. What was that doing here? Did Brett Moody leave it here? Or Beth Pinsky?

Jinx heard bicycle wheels. Allie, Liz, and Delia biked up. Delia stared at Moody Manor with her mouth open.

"It's bigger than our school!" she said.

Liz and Allie had plastic bags slung over their handlebars.

"We have the lobsters," said Liz. "I guess we should bring them up to the house."

They all looked toward the house. The front door opened, and The Beautiful Marla came out with Clay behind her.

"Who's that guy?" asked Delia.

"That's Clay," Jinx said. "I see he just met Marla. Does he look like a movie star to you?" he asked.

"Or a crook!" said Delia.

"Or a country singer," said Allie.

Maybe that was why the Texans could stay in Maine all summer! Clay flew back and forth to act or sing! But no, Jinx remembered; Lee said ROY flew back and forth. CLAY stayed with the boys.

Lester came back around the house with an ax. He stared at Marla. Clay called to him. He shook his head. Now Roy crowded into the doorway.

"What are they going to do to her?" asked Allie.

"She's going to jail!" said Delia.

Jinx heard a shout. "No," he said, "It's something else."

Marla escaped. She got on her bike and raced down the drive to them.

"Have you guys seen Lee and Sonny?" she called.

"Not for a while," said Jinx.

"Urchin Cave!" said Allie.

She dropped her bike, lobsters and all. She raced for the shore. Liz, Marla, and Delia raced after her. Jinx stopped long enough to grab the rope. When he reached the top of the rocks, he gasped.

There was Lee, standing out on the farthest rock! The ocean crashed at his feet.

He had his arms up, shouting with glee.

"Tide's coming in!" said Allie. "If we don't get him off there, he'll be swept away!"

"I'll get those men!" shouted Delia.

She raced off. Jinx and Allie climbed down the rocks.

"Lee!" shouted Jinx. "Come back!"

But Lee couldn't hear him. The sound of crashing waves was too loud. Jinx watched a wave smash into Lee's rock. Lee laughed. The water level rose. Now there was water all around Lee's rock.

"Lee!" called a louder voice. It was Sonny's. He climbed out of Urchin Cave and worked his way toward Lee. Jinx shouted again. If Sonny didn't watch out, he'd be swept off too!

Lee turned around. He saw that water surrounded him. His face turned white.

Jinx and Allie reached Sonny's side.

"Here's a rope!" Jinx cried.

Sonny grabbed it. He threw one end toward his brother. Lee reached for it and missed. Sonny cast it again. A wave caught

Lee in the back of the legs. He missed the rope.

"Make a chain!" Jinx shouted.

He stood behind Sonny on the slippery rock. He wrapped his arms around Sonny's waist from behind. Allie stood behind Jinx. She wrapped her arms around him.

Marla and Liz scrambled down the rocks. Marla wrapped herself around Allie. Liz held onto Marla.

Sonny cast the rope again. This time Lee caught it.

"Hold on!" shouted Sonny.

Another wave caught Lee. It swept him off the rock. Jinx heard the men shout and Delia scream from the rocks above. He felt Sonny heave hard on the rope. Salty water splashed Jinx's ankles. He heard the girls gasp when the water hit them. But no one let go.

Lee bobbed in the water. But he held on to the rope. The salty waves washed him toward the rocks.

"Come on!" yelled Sonny. "Come on!"

"Rope him in, Sonny!" they heard Roy shout.

A huge wave boomed up. It crashed with

a roar. White foam broke. Water rushed around Jinx's ankles. He felt it tugging at his feet. It wanted to pull him off the rock and out to sea.

If the ocean had its way, they'd all fall in!

7
RESCUE!

Lee's western hat washed past Jinx's legs. Jinx was afraid to look for Lee. He felt Sonny bend suddenly. Lee had washed against the rock in front of them. Sonny kept hold of the rope with one hand. He grabbed Lee's shirt with the other. The ocean tried to pull Lee back.

Jinx held onto Sonny. Allie held onto Jinx. Liz and Marla reached out to grab Lee's arm. They all hauled backward until Lee landed on the rock beside them. Another wave boomed at them.

"We've got to get out of here!" shouted Allie.

The men reached them. Roy and Clay grabbed Lee. Lester helped the rest of them up to dry rock. A wave caught The Beautiful Marla and soaked her. Her clothes clung to her. Jinx grinned. Sonny helped her to dry ground.

"You did it! You saved him!" shouted Delia.

"It was close," said Allie.

Lester ran for his truck. He and Roy lifted Lee into the front seat. Lester drove them up to Moody Manor. Clay, Sonny, and Marla followed on foot. Clay waved to the kids.

"Come back to the house," he called.

"He's scary!" whispered Delia.

"I wonder if he wears those sunglasses to

bed," said Allie.

"Maybe his eyes hurt," said Delia.

"The lobsters!" cried Liz suddenly. "We left them in the grass!"

They ran to get the plastic bags. One of the lobsters had crawled out.

"Escape! Escape!" cried Jinx.

He grabbed the dark brown creature. It waved its claws. It couldn't grab him, though. Gramp had put pegs in its claws.

"Poor things," said Liz. "Maybe we should let them go. To thank the ocean for giving Lee back."

"Yes!" said Delia.

"Don't be dumb," said Jinx.

He put the lobster back in the bag. Lobsters had to be boiled alive. Liz couldn't stand that. She never ate them. Jinx didn't think about it. Food was food.

"Where's the kitchen?" asked Allie when they reached the house.

"Back there," said Jinx.

He led the girls down the long hall. Their feet squished in their wet shoes. The portraits stared down at them, as if all the dead Moodys wanted to yell at their wet footprints.

Clay stood next to the warm oven. He still had his wet boots on, and his sunglasses. Delia stuck close to Liz. Liz and

Jinx put the bags of lobsters into the refrigerator.

"Where's Lee?" Allie asked.

"In front of the fireplace," said Clay. "Y'all go on in there. I'm making a brew of hot lemon and honey. And I don't want any help. Go on."

Maybe Clay didn't want any of them to recognize him from the WANTED posters. Clay's sunglasses stared right at Jinx.

"Git," Clay growled.

They found Lee in the smallest living room. He had two blankets wrapped tightly around him. A fire leaped in the fireplace. Jinx put his sneakers on the hearth to dry.

"How's it going, bud?" he asked.

Lee tried to smile. "I'll live," he said. "Thanks to you guys."

"This is Allie Davies," said Jinx, "Delia Clark, and my cousin Liz French. Allie's the one who remembered Urchin Cave."

"My whole family loves to go there," said Allie. "It was easy to guess."

Allie had three brothers and one sister. All the Davies kids were adopted. They came from Korea, the U.S., Colombia, the Ukraine, and Guatemala.

"Maine tides go up and down nine to twelve feet around here," Allie told Lee.

"And we just had a storm," Delia added. "That makes the tides worse."

"I guess!" said Lee.

"Did you know the cave was down there?" asked Jinx. He wanted to know if it was marked on a smuggler's map.

"Pa said the right place would have a cave," said Lee.

"What right place?" asked Jinx.

Lee didn't answer. "Is Marla your sister?" he asked Liz.

"Yes," said Liz. "But it isn't my fault."

"Hey!" said Delia with a frown.

Lee laughed.

"Where IS Marla?" asked Delia.

"Pa took her upstairs to get her some dry clothes." said Lee.

"Oh, boy!" muttered Liz.

"Let's go too!" cried Delia.

The girls went upstairs, leaving Jinx alone with Lee. Jinx grabbed his chance.

"I can tell you guys are looking for something," he said. "Let us help! Maybe we already know where to find what you're looking for!"

Lee shook his head. "I can't say," he said. "I promised."

"How about if I just guess?" asked Jinx. "You don't have to say anything. If I'm right, you can signal."

Lee's eyes gleamed.

"You have a map," guessed Jinx. "A smuggler's map? A pirate's map?"

Lee didn't move. No map? Rats!

"Okay," said Jinx. "But you're looking for a certain place, right? A house?"

Lee's eyebrows went up. That looked like a "maybe."

"Or something around a house?" guessed Jinx. "Like a cave? Or a...tree?"

Lee sighed. Like Jinx had gotten close, then missed the point.

Jinx frowned. "Maybe it's more than one thing," he thought out loud.

Lee's eyes went wide open. That was it! Lee and his family were looking for more than one thing! Jinx leaned forward.

"Is it treasure?" he asked. Maybe the treasure was divided up and buried in different places!

Lee just laughed, like Jinx's idea was a

good joke. Jinx heard footsteps. There was something else he just had to know.

"Is your uncle an outlaw?" he asked.

Lee laughed again. Too hard. Jinx wished he'd kept quiet. He felt stupid.

Everyone came downstairs. Marla looked like the perfect cowgirl. She had on a western style shirt and Sonny's jeans. Delia gazed at her with awe.

"Doing okay, boy?" Roy asked Lee.

Lee nodded.

"You're sure lucky to get away with just a little chill," said Roy. "I don't want you roaming over those rocks without me, you hear? Forget the twisted paths and angry stones. There will be time enough to find them this summer."

Twisted paths! Angry stones! Jinx's heart beat fast. Clues! He could look for them while he worked!

"I'm going to get y'all something warm to drink," said Roy.

He left. Marla took center stage.

"Moody Manor is haunted," she said.

Delia squeaked.

"Is that right?" said Sonny.

Jinx hid a grin.

"I heard the ghost myself," Marla said. "When my cousin Mike brought me here."

Jinx had to bite the inside of his mouth to keep from laughing out loud. Liz looked at him. She put one eyebrow up. She always gave Jinx a look when Marla got carried away.

"Is it true, Jinx?" asked Lee. "Is the place haunted?'

"Didn't Lester tell you?" said Jinx. "Haunted by the ghost of the man who last owned it!"

Delia squeaked again. Allie kicked Jinx on the ankle. But Jinx was enjoying himself too much to care. Lee's eyes gleamed.

"Let's stay up all night and find that ghost," he said to Sonny.

Roy came in with a tray. "Lemon tea and pecan cookies," he said.

"Pa," said Lee. "Jinx says Moody Manor has a ghost."

"Is that right?" said Roy.

He and Sonny and Lee all looked at Jinx. Clay came in. He looked at Jinx, too, through his sunglasses.

"Marla started it!" Jinx wanted to say.

"Maybe Jinx should come spend the night here," said Clay. "And help y'all find that ghost."

Jinx's heart leaped. He knew there was no ghost! But maybe he could find out what the Texans were looking for! Or why Clay was in hiding! Then he remembered Drew.

"I'd like to spend the night, sir," he said. "But I can't. I asked my friend Drew Ellis to spend the night with me."

"Let him come," said Roy. "We've got room enough. Right, boys?"

He and the boys looked at one another. Jinx saw some kind of secret signal pass between them.

But what did it mean?

8

THE ANGRY STONE

Jinx went back to work. The girls stopped to talk to him before they biked home.

"I told Sonny his Uncle Clay looked sort of famous," said Marla. "And Sonny got mad!"

"Yes," said Delia. "Like that was the worst thing Marla could say!"

"Maybe Clay really IS in hiding," said Allie.

"Maybe I'll find out tonight," said Jinx.

"And Jinx," said Liz, "check out the smallest bedroom! It has a pile of portraits in it!"

"There are portraits everywhere," said Jinx.

"But these aren't hanging up!" said Liz. "They're stacked against the bed."

"So?" said Jinx.

"Just look at them," said Allie. "We want to know if you see what we saw."

"Later. I don't have time now," Jinx said. He got to work hauling brush. Then Roy drove him to Rocky Point. He wanted to meet Jinx's and Drew's parents. While Roy talked to Mom and Dad, Jinx got his stuff together. He packed a bedroll and his pj's. He added a wooden ball from a lawn game and an empty glass bottle. He planned to have a little fun with Lee and Sonny!

Next, Jinx showed Roy the way to Drew's house. They had to go through "town," the busy part of Ragged Island, near the ferry landing. Drew lived south of town, on the road to Spruce Mountain. Drew's mom was a veterinarian. The Ellises had an animal shelter attached to their house.

While Roy talked to Drew's mom, Jinx

told Drew Gramp's story about Earl Moody. He told him about his talk with Lee, Mike's movie set idea, and the rescue at Urchin Cave.

"I wish I'd been there!" said Drew.

"We'll have fun tonight," said Jinx. "You can help me haunt Lee and Sonny!"

Drew's mom agreed to the overnight, and Roy drove them back to Moody Manor.

"I want y'all to make yourselves at home," said Roy. "I owe my son's life to you, Jinx, and I won't forget it."

Clay didn't say any such thing, though. He just nodded when Roy introduced Drew. Jinx could swear there was an almost-smile on Clay's face. Not a friendly smile—a GOTCHA smile. Had Lee told Clay that Jinx thought Clay was a crook? Lee and Sonny looked friendly, though. Jinx could tell they'd all get along fine.

"I want to look around outside," said Sonny.

"I feel all right, Pa," said Lee. "Let me go too."

"I guess it's okay," said Roy. "Just stay away from the rocks!"

Jinx felt better when they got outside, away from Clay.

"That was fast thinking your friends did this morning," Sonny told Drew. "They saved my brother. Me too, I guess. Where did you get that rope, Jinx?"

"Found it in the bushes." said Jinx.

"Is that right?' said Sonny. "Funny place for a rope."

"Unless you plan to use it for breaking into a house," said Drew.

He and Jinx told Sonny and Lee about the hinge, the open window, and what they'd found under the gazebo.

"The second floor has a few broken window latches too," said Sonny. "This place needs a guard dog. Or a shotgun."

Jinx hoped Sonny was kidding about the gun. Maybe Clay had one.

"Have you seen the gazebo?" Drew asked.

"Yeah," said Sonny. "Looks like it goes on a wedding cake. What I want to check out is that wall of hedges. Why do you think someone planted them? For a fence?"

"It's a puzzle hedge," said Drew.

"What do you mean?" asked Lee.

"It's a maze," said Jinx. "And we're the rats!"

"Has it been here long?" asked Sonny.

"Over a hundred years," said Drew. "It takes time to grow hedges that tall."

"Hmm," said Sonny. He didn't explain why he'd asked.

The hedges made a thick, high wall. The boys followed along it until they found an opening. A short path led into the maze. They filed in.

"Weird," said Jinx.

For some reason, he had to whisper. Hedges lined both sides of the path. They were high, as tall as the walls inside Moody Manor. The path ended, and the boys had to choose which way to turn.

"Let's go left," said Lee.

They went deeper into the maze. Jinx wondered if these were Roy's "twisted paths." Some paths twisted. Some were straight. But every one was either a dead end or a corner turn.

"You could get lost easy," said Drew.

"Yeah," said Jinx. He was glad he wasn't in here by himself. He wasn't sure he could get out.

They got to a round, open space. Four benches faced a stone statue in the center.

"The angry eagle!" shouted Lee.

It was like he knew about it already! Sonny didn't say a word, but his eyes glittered. Jinx took a good look at the angry eagle. Was there a treasure map hidden in there? But Lee and Sonny weren't looking for a treasure map. They were looking for a way out of the maze.

"We have to tell Pa!" said Sonny. "But I

92

can't tell which path we took!"

"We came from THAT path," said Drew. "I think."

"We'd better try them one by one," said Jinx. "And stick together!"

Sonny headed down one of the paths. Three turns, and they reached a dead end.

"We should have a bag of crumbs," said Jinx. "Like Hansel and Gretel."

He tried another path. He saw a red flash at the end of it.

"Hey!" he shouted. "Come back here!"

But whoever it was turned a corner and disappeared.

"That's Brett Moody!" said Drew.

They chased after him. The path ended, and they had to choose again.

"You two go that way!" said Sonny. "We'll go this way!"

Jinx and Drew's path ended in another

choice—a three-way choice this time. Jinx peered down each path. He saw no red shirt anywhere; just green hedge.

"Shh!" said Drew.

Jinx heard running footsteps—too many for just one person. After a moment Lee and Sonny appeared.

"Our way was a dead end!" said Lee. "Did you catch him?"

"No," said Drew.

"Is there something secret inside that statue?" asked Jinx. "Something someone might want to steal?"

"In the statue?" said Lee. "Naw! It's—"

Sonny poked him in the back. Lee shut up. Jinx and Drew looked at each other.

"Let's try to get out of here," said Jinx.

They took a wrong turn and found Brett Moody in a dead-end path, trying to look like he wasn't there.

"Well, well," said Sonny. "Maybe we found the owner of the rope."

"What do you know?" said Brett.

"Did you use it to get into the house?" asked Lee.

"I never took anything, and you can't prove I did!" said Brett. "I just wanted to get inside!" He looked at Drew. "My family could be living in this place! We're Moodys. And no one else is living here."

"Never mind," said Sonny. "Your rope came in handy. We used it to haul my brother out of the ocean. Now, get going, and we'll forget we saw you."

Brett couldn't get going. He didn't know the way out any more than Jinx did.

Jinx almost felt sorry for him. "Let's all leave together," he said. That way there would be no chance to lose Brett, and no chance for him to hide out in the Puzzle Hedge.

It took them about twenty tries, but they finally made it out. Right away Brett broke into a run. He crashed into the woods. Lee and Sonny forgot all about him. They rushed to the house.

"Lee and Sonny were looking for that eagle!" Jinx said to Drew. "But why?"

"Beats me," said Drew. "But I don't think they're scouting for a movie set!"

"Me neither," said Jinx. "And I was thinking. ROY is looking for someplace particular. But CLAY thinks Roy is nuts— remember? We heard him say so yesterday, at the stables!"

"Right!" said Drew. "What CLAY wants is to be someplace out of the way!"

"So there are TWO things going on," said Jinx. "ROY'S looking for a particular place. And CLAY wants to be where no one knows him!"

"Man," said Drew. "What if Clay is dangerous? We better not let him know we've been wondering about him!"

Jinx heard a door slam.

"That's the same sound I heard yesterday!" he told Drew. "Just before Liz and Allie got here!"

"Listen!" said Drew.

Shouts came from the trees Brett had run

into. Those woods separated the Moody Manor property from Rim Road.

"That's Brett!" said Drew. "Come on!"

9

Secrets Revealed

They ran toward the voices. Sticks snapped under their feet, but the voices kept on shouting. The boys got close enough to see Beth Pinsky's truck through the trees and to hear Brett Moody and Beth Pinsky yelling at each other.

"Don't think you'll get away with it!" yelled Beth Pinsky. "I know you've been breaking in there, poking and prying as if the place was already yours!"

"So what?" said Brett. "And how would you know? Unless you've been doing the same thing?"

"I saw that open window yesterday!" yelled Beth. "And I have as much right to be there as you have! I'm a Moody on my mother's side!"

"Mind your own business!" said Brett.

He pulled a bike out of its hiding place. He leaped on it and pedaled away. Beth Pinsky slammed her fist onto the hood of her truck. Then she turned around and stared up at the roof of Moody Manor.

"It will never be mine," she

said. She sounded like she'd just lost her dog.

Jinx had to know more. He shot through the bushes.

"Ms. Pinsky," he said. "Did you really lose a hammer?"

Beth Pinsky scowled when she saw him. She looked scared too.

"You!" she said. "What are you doing here? I suppose you heard me argue with Brett! Are you going to tattle to Lester?"

"If there's something Lester should know, you should be the one to tell him," said Drew.

"Ms. Pinsky," said Jinx. "Did you leave a window open on the third floor of Moody Manor?"

Beth Pinsky's shoulders slumped.

"I broke the latch on a first floor window last winter," she said. "When I was in there

101

working with Lester. I never thought about Moody Manor before I got inside. It's such a great old house! Lester told me about the court dispute, and I got to thinking. My mother is a Moody! Why couldn't Moody Manor belong to us?"

"Why did you break the window latch?" asked Drew.

"So I could get in again," said Beth. "I just wanted to look around! One day after I got inside, I found Brett in there too! We scared each other half to death."

Despite herself, she smiled. Jinx liked her better.

"I didn't lose a hammer," she said. "That was just an excuse. I knew Liz saw me yesterday. She and your other friend ran by me just as I realized I'd left the window open on the third floor."

"You were inside Moody Manor

yesterday?" asked Jinx. "When I got there?"

"I saw you crash into that bush," said Beth Pinsky.

This time her smile went ear to ear.

"How do you get in?" asked Drew.

"I step on the branches of a bush under the window," said Beth. "I push the window open and pull myself up."

"But what about the third floor window?" asked Jinx.

"You two were working too close to where I get in," said Beth. "So I dropped down to the roof of the wing and slid down the drainpipe to the ground. Then I took the long way back to my truck—through the woods. I had reached it just before Liz ran by."

"I heard you," said Jinx.

The door slam—that was Beth getting into her truck.

Beth sighed. "I'll go see Lester right now," she said, "and confess. I know it was wrong. And I was only dreaming, anyhow. Moody Manor will never belong to me."

She got into her truck and pulled away.

"So that solves one mystery!" said Jinx. "We know who's been breaking into Moody Manor!"

"We had better get back to the house," said Drew. "They're probably wondering what happened to us."

It didn't look like any of the Trues had missed them. Lee and Sonny were in the little living room, talking to Roy. Their voices were quiet, but excited. The talk stopped when Jinx and Drew came in. Roy put on a cartoon smile.

"Sounds like you boys had another adventure," he drawled. "Y'all have had quite a day!"

"You can say that again!" said Jinx. "We just found out who's been breaking into Moody Manor!"

He and Drew told about Beth Pinsky.

"That's one puzzle solved," said Roy. "Now we're fixing to make y'all some good food, Texas style," said Roy. "Why don't you two go on upstairs? Scout around. Pick out where you want to sleep tonight."

Jinx wanted to stay and listen to the talk. But they had no choice. He and Drew went upstairs.

"He wanted us out of there!" said Drew.

"No kidding!" said Jinx. "But it's okay. We can plan the haunting!"

Their overnight stuff was on the upstairs landing. Jinx took out the wooden ball and the glass bottle. Then he and Drew went up to the top floor. They looked in all the bedrooms. One was full of boxes. One had

105

only a dresser. The one on the end was best.
It looked out on the ocean.

"A good place for ghosts," said Drew.

Jinx felt it too. "This is the room for us!"
he said. "Let's plant ghost stuff!"

He opened a door in the corner of the
room. He expected a closet. But the door led
into the little room next door. That room
was empty too. Jinx opened the door from
there to the hall. That door creaked.

"Here's our ghost!" said Jinx.

"Sounds like a door to me," said Drew.

Jinx closed the door. He opened it again,
slowly. This time the creak was spookier.

"Better," said Drew.

Jinx put down the wooden ball he held.
It rolled. It made a great sound, like a giant's
stomach rumbling.

"They'll hear it!" said Drew.

"They're two floors down!" said Jinx. But

he set the wooden ball in a corner of the room, for later use.

"What's the bottle for?" asked Drew.

Jinx held the top of the bottle in front of his lips. He blew across it. Drew nodded. The bottle made a whoo-oo sound. Like a ghost, howling.

"Ready!" said Jinx. "Now to stay awake after Lee and Sonny fall asleep!"

Jinx and Drew took a quick look through the second floor. The rooms here had plenty of furniture. The smallest one was pretty cluttered, thanks to the framed portraits leaning against the walls and bed. Jinx remembered that Liz and Allie wanted him to look at them. He didn't, though. It was time to get back downstairs.

Lee, Sonny, and Roy were still talking. They looked up, all smiles, when Jinx and Drew came in.

Jinx glanced at Drew. Something was up.

"Dinner's almost ready," said Roy. "We thought we might as well make use of that fine big dining room! We got it all set up. And we lit us a fire."

A good thing too. It was dark out now. The April night was cold.

"Food's on!" called Clay from the kitchen.

Was he the cook? Jinx hoped he wouldn't poison them or drug them into not waking up till morning!

"Can we help?" asked Drew.

"No, no," said Roy. "You're our guests of honor! Y'all just go on into the dining room and take a seat."

Jinx would feel better if he could be sure Clay wasn't drugging the food.

It took two tries to find the dining room. There were no lights on in there, just candles. Jinx couldn't see anything out the windows. There WAS nothing out there, except night and the ocean. He and Drew took the two seats on one side of the long table. Jinx felt like he should whisper.

Roy came in with a big tray. Five boiled lobsters lay on it. They were bright red now. The others carried things in too. Clay had a big pot. It smelled spicy.

"Texas barbecue," said Roy.

The barbecue was hotter than Aunt Jean's chili. Jinx loved it. He liked food that made him feel like steam was coming out of his

109

ears. For a while no one talked. They just ate. They ate by candlelight, and firelight, like in the good old days. Clay had his hat off, but not his sunglasses.

"Well, boys," said Roy, "what can you tell us about this big house, hmm? You must know a story about it."

"You mean, besides that it's haunted?" said Jinx.

He meant to lighten things up, but no one laughed.

"Besides that," said Roy.

"Well," said Jinx, "this place belongs to Lester Moody's brother. Earl."

"Earl?" said Lee. He looked like he'd just found the angry eagle again.

There was a loud silence. Jinx looked at Drew. Maybe the Texans DID know an Earl! They just didn't know that Earl was a Moody!

"Where IS this Earl?" asked Clay.

Clay's voice was quiet. But somehow it told Jinx to answer NOW.

"No one knows," said Jinx.

Lee and Sonny looked at each other. Roy and Clay stared at Jinx.

"Earl's been missing for something like thirty-five years," explained Drew. "The last place they saw him was—"

"Yes?" said Clay, softly.

"Texas," finished Jinx.

Lee gasped. Then he winced. Like Sonny had stomped on his foot.

"So this place is Lester's now, right?" said Roy.

"Lester takes care of it," said Drew. "But there's a pile of Moodys after it."

"Like the one we met in the hedge maze," said Sonny. "He seems to think HE should be living here now."

Jinx didn't like the way Sonny talked about Brett. After all, Brett lived on Ragged Island. Sonny didn't.

"I don't care who gets the house," said Jinx. "I just wish Lester knew what happened to Earl. I would hate it if my brother Mike were missing and I didn't know what happened to him."

Lee and Sonny and Clay looked at Roy. A funny look crossed Roy's face. Like he knew something about missing brothers.

"Let's talk about something more cheerful," Roy said. He smiled the cartoon smile at Jinx and Drew. "Like ghosts."

"Okay!" said Jinx brightly. "Moody Manor's ghost lives on the third floor, on the ocean side." He decided he better not say it was Earl Moody's ghost.

"I THOUGHT there was something about the third floor!" said Clay. His voice rose.

"Didn't I tell you, Roy? Didn't I? I went up to that floor, and I felt something cold against my face!"

The way Clay said "cold" made Jinx shiver. He stared at Clay's sunglasses. You mean there was a REAL ghost up there?

"I know you said so, Clay," said Roy. He said it like Clay was a little kid.

Jinx wished he could see Clay's eyes.

"Guess we better sleep up on the third floor," said Sonny, "if we want to see a ghost for ourselves."

Sonny, Lee, Roy, and Clay's sunglasses all turned to look at Jinx and Drew. Jinx felt the back of his neck get cold. He stood up. What did they know that they weren't telling?

10
GHOST STORIES

After dinner was cleaned up, the boys dragged mattresses into the end room on the top floor. Jinx and Drew spread bedrolls on two of them. Sonny and Lee brought blankets and pillows up from the second floor.

Roy brought up a couple of flashlights. "No electric lights up here tonight," he said. "Ghosts don't like 'em. Clay will be up in a bit. Meanwhile, maybe Jinx can tell us about the Moody Manor ghost."

Roy sat on the edge of Lee's mattress. Everybody looked at Jinx.

Show time! Jinx made his voice spooky.

"First of all, this place stood empty for years," he said. "See, everyone expected Earl to come home someday. The rooms

inside looked just the same as the day Earl's father died.

"His slippers were by the bed. The book he was reading was open face down. When they couldn't find Earl anywhere, Lester closed Moody Manor up tight. For years, not even he came inside."

Jinx cleared his throat. "Finally the courts said Lester could rent the place out summers. When Lester came inside, he found everything just the way he left it. Except all the portraits were turned to the wall." Jinx paused. "And then Lester heard footsteps. Up here. On the third floor."

Lee's eyes were wide. But Sonny looked bored. Like he was listening to "The Three Little Kittens."

Drew spoke up. Jinx tried not to look surprised.

"Lester heard dog footsteps too," said

Drew. "But he didn't have a dog."

What dog? Jinx waited for Drew to go on. Drew didn't. Jinx thought fast.

"EARL used to have a dog," he said. "A mutt named Digger. Lester thought of Digger when he heard those dog steps. He whistled. He heard a dog running. Then he heard a howl. And a kind of WHOOSHING sound. Like wind being sucked OUT of the house—backwards!"

Lee's mouth dropped open. Roy's eyes gleamed. Jinx began to enjoy himself.

"All the curtains fluttered," he said. "A portrait fell off the wall. Lester ran up the stairs. But when he got up here, he found no one. No man. No ghost. No dog. Only an open window."

Clay came down the hall. At least Jinx hoped it was Clay. SOMEONE'S boots made loud, slow sounds. At last Clay appeared.

The collar of his shirt was open. His hair looked wild.

"I can feel it, Roy!" he cried. "I tell you, I can FEEL it!"

Feel what? Wind rattled the old windows. Jinx got goosebumps. Maybe there really was a ghost!

"It's an empty feeling," said Clay. "Like something left this place behind." His voice rose. "And it's trying to come back! It wants to get back in!"

119

Yikes! Maybe it wasn't Clay who was in hiding! Maybe Roy and the boys hid him! Because he was some kind of nut!

"Settle down, little brother," said Roy in a soft voice.

"Yeah, Uncle Clay," said Lee "It's all right. We're here."

Clay shook his head like a wet dog. Sonny got to his feet.

"Don't get riled up, Uncle Clay," he said. "You know it's bad for you."

He took Clay's arm. Gently. Jinx held his breath.

"I'm not riled," said Clay. "I'm calm."

"Right," thought Jinx. "And I'm the president."

Clay turned to Jinx and Drew. Jinx stared up into his sunglasses.

"I know things," said Clay.

Now he SOUNDED like an evil robot, too.

His voice was soft, with breath all around his words.

"I know when someone who used to live in a house tries to get back inside. They do it all the time, the dead ones. The unhappy dead."

Jinx's teeth began to chatter. He tried to tell himself it was the cold air creeping in around the old windows.

"That's why sometimes I DO things," whispered Clay. "Things the unhappy dead tell me to do."

Now Roy was on his feet.

"That's enough, Clay," he said. "Y'all are scaring the boys. Let's go downstairs and let them be."

He and Sonny led Clay out. Clay went, muttering. Jinx swallowed.

"Is your uncle okay?" Drew asked Lee.

"He gets a little strange sometimes," said

Lee. "We have to keep an eye on him. But don't worry. Dad will stay with him."

Jinx crawled into his sleeping bag. The ghosts of Moody Manor didn't need any help from him! It felt like the place was already haunted! If not by Earl Moody's ghost, then by the living Clay True.

Jinx planned to stay awake so he could haunt Lee and Sonny. But he fell asleep, then woke up with a start. What time was it? Jinx couldn't tell. He heard sleeping all around him, though. At least Clay hadn't drugged the food. That was something. Maybe someone should have drugged CLAY'S food.

Jinx pinched Drew. "They're asleep!" he breathed in Drew's ear. "Get up!"

Drew came wide awake. He slid out of his bedroll. They listened a minute to be sure they hadn't woken Lee and Sonny. Then they crept to the door in the corner and slipped into the next room. Jinx closed the door between the rooms.

"We made it!" he whispered.

It was too dark to see Drew's face, but Jinx could feel the grin on his own. He felt for the wooden ball and rolled it across the floor. The house was so quiet, it sounded like a cannonball. Drew must have grabbed the bottle; Jinx heard a hollow "whoooo."

Then the door to the hall creaked open. The ghost?

Clay! Holding a lit candle! And standing in the doorway looking as angry as the stone eagle!

11

The Secret of Moody Manor

"YI!" shouted Jinx. He couldn't help it. Drew dropped the bottle. The door from the bedroom opened. It let in a flashlight beam. A horrible sound rose up.

Laughter.

"Gotcha!" cried Roy's voice.

"Oh boy, was that fun!" cried Lee's voice. "Uncle Clay sure had you going!"

Drew caught on before Jinx did.

"You mean we thought WE were

spooking YOU," said Drew, "and all the time YOU were spooking US?"

"Right!" said Sonny. "It was Uncle Clay's idea!"

The overhead light came on. So did Jinx's brain.

"I bet I know when he got that idea," said Jinx. "When Lee told him I asked if Clay was a crook."

"That's about it," drawled Clay.

He was smiling. But Jinx still wished he could see Clay's eyes.

"What gave you that idea, anyhow?" asked Roy. "That Clay's a crook?"

"The sunglasses," said Jinx.

"I figured," said Clay.

"Why do you wear them?" asked Jinx.

"That's a story for another day," said Clay. "Let's get down to the real story. Let's go downstairs where there's a warm fire.

We'll tell you what we're looking for. Maybe together we can solve the mystery of Moody Manor."

They gathered in a cheerful living room in front of a fireplace.

"Shall I tell the story, Roy?" asked Clay. "Or will you?"

"I'll tell it," said Roy. "After all, it's my story." He looked at Jinx and Drew. "My mother, Ruby, married Wayne True when I was two years old. Soon my little brother, Clay, came along. And we were a happy family. But I always knew the man I called Daddy wasn't my father. Mama refused to speak about my father. She was too mad at him. Because one day he left home and never came back."

Jinx's heart began to race. He had an idea who Roy's father might be!

"Mama told stories about a big house.

She said it was built by a merchant seaman. There was a gazebo for summer parties. There were twisted paths and a stone statue.

It was an angry statue, to chase away bad people. The house stood right on the ocean on an island off the coast of Maine."

Jinx had to ask a question. "Did she say your father had lived there?" he asked.

Roy shook his head. "I never put Mama's stories together with my father. I thought she made the place up."

"I got to thinking that maybe the place was real," said Clay. "And maybe Roy's father had told Mama about it."

"So that's why you started coming to Maine islands," said Drew. "To look for the place your mother talked about?"

"Yes. And because I hoped I'd learn more about my father. The one thing Mama told me about him was his name."

"Earl!" guessed Jinx.

"Earl," said Roy.

"No kidding!" said Drew.

"I'm named for him," said Sonny. "Sonny's my nickname."

"That's right," said Roy. "I named Sonny Earl. Because I never believed my father left us. I think something happened to him, and he COULDN'T come back."

"Maybe Earl Moody is your father," said Drew.

"I'd like to think so," said Roy. "But I wish I had more than a few stories to go on. I wish I had proof."

Jinx remembered something.

"The portraits!" he cried. "Liz told me to look at some portraits she saw upstairs yesterday! Maybe there's a clue up there!"

They all went upstairs. Jinx hurried into the little bedroom. He pulled out the

129

portraits, one by one.

They all saw it at the same time.

"Lee!" shouted Sonny. He grabbed the framed painting from Jinx's hands. "This one looks just like YOU!"

It did, too. The young man in the portrait had straight, thick eyebrows. Just like Lee's.

"Who is this guy?" asked Lee.

"We can ask Lester!" said Sonny. "Right, Pa?"

But Roy wasn't listening. He picked up another portrait.

It was the painting of a woman. She had a smile full of secrets. And thick, dark eyebrows, like Lee's.

"Who's that?" asked Drew.

Roy put the portrait down. He took a wallet out of his back pocket. He pulled an old, faded photo out of the wallet and held the photo up by the portrait.

It was the woman in the painting.

"This photo belonged to my father," said Roy. "Mama wanted to throw it away. But my daddy, Wayne True, saved it for me. Said it might be all I ever had of my father's family."

"It's her," said Clay. "I'd bet on it."

"Lester will know who she is!" said Jinx.

Roy put an arm around each of his sons.

"Well, boys," he said, "maybe we're home."

12

ANSWERED QUESTIONS

Everyone got up early. Who could sleep? They gathered in the kitchen to watch Clay make pancakes. Sonny brought the portrait of the mystery woman downstairs. Roy took the electric clock off the kitchen wall. He hung the woman's portrait in its place.

Someone knocked on the kitchen door. Lester already? Jinx yanked the door open. It was The Beautiful Marla, with two coffee cakes. She stepped right past him.

"Ma sent these," Marla half sang. "Because you had Jinx and Drew overnight!"

Right. Jinx knew Marla brought them because she had to see Sonny. Jinx didn't close the door yet because Liz was in the yard with Allie Davies and Delia Clark.

"Delia came to see Marla," said Liz. "Allie came over for coffee cake. We decided to come eat it here."

Lee joined Jinx at the door.

"Looks like a party," he said. "Y'all better come on in. Uncle Clay's making pancakes."

"Pancakes!" said Delia.

No one had to tell her twice. She rushed past Jinx.

"I guess you found the portraits," said Liz when she got inside.

"That woman looks just like Lee!" said Marla. She looked from the portrait to Lee's face. "Did you bring that painting with you from Texas?"

The boys began to fill the girls in. They told about the angry eagle, and finding Brett in the puzzle hedge. Then they told all about the hauntings, Roy's missing father, the portraits, and Roy's photo.

"But Clay still won't tell us why he wears sunglasses," said Jinx.

"I have a guess," said Liz softly.

Another knock sounded on the kitchen door. It was Lester.

"Just the man I wanted to see!" said Roy. "Come on in."

"I thought I'd drop by," said Lester. "See if you needed anything."

He turned to shut the door. Delia looked at Lee.

"If it wasn't for the gray hair," she said, "I'd think that was your dad."

Jinx remembered that the day before

135

he'd mistaken Lester for Roy. No wonder! From the back they looked just alike!

Sonny pulled out a chair for Lester. If Lester sat in it, he'd be facing the wall and the portrait of the woman.

"Have a seat," said Roy.

Lester sat down. "Looks like the whole island's come for breakfast," he said. He glanced up over Delia's head—at the portrait of the woman.

"I had that portrait set aside in the little bedroom," he said, "with the other paintings I plan to keep for myself."

"Who is it?" asked Lee.

"That's my mother, Thelma," said Lester.

"And Earl's mother?" asked Jinx.

Lester nodded. "What's it hanging down here for?" he asked.

Roy took out his photo. "This belonged to my father," he said. He handed the photo to

Lester. "The only other thing I know about my father is that his name was Earl."

Lester looked at the photo. There was a long silence.

"I have this picture too," he said at last. "It's Ma." He stood up so fast his chair fell over. "You're my nephew!" he said to Roy. "You're family!"

Jinx heard Liz sniff.

"It's so romantic!" said Marla.

"They're so lucky," whispered Allie.

All the Texans hugged Lester.

Jinx thought the family reunion was great. But there were still two things he wanted to know.

"What happened to Earl Moody?" he asked.

Clay came over and sat down between Jinx and Drew. "My daddy, Wayne True, always thought Earl was lost at sea."

"That's right," said Roy. "He used to fish on the Gulf of Mexico."

"I always figured my brother was lost at sea too," said Lester. "Earl belonged on water, not on land. As far back as I can remember, he was always in a boat, sailing. OR fishing. He couldn't be a lawyer like Dad wanted. He and Dad didn't get along, but I always thought Earl would get in touch with me. I still miss him. But finding his sons and grandsons! That's almost as good as finding Earl."

He and Roy sat down to talk. Sonny and Lee pulled chairs up close by. Delia eyed the coffee cakes.

"I'm hungry," she said.

"Guess I'll make some pancakes!" said Clay.

"Wait," said Jinx. "Please, could you answer one more question for me? ARE you in hiding?"

"Sort of," said Clay.

"It's your face, isn't it?" asked Liz gently. "Were you in an accident?"

"A real bad car accident," said Clay. "My face got burned. And that cut short my acting career."

"You're an ACTOR!" said The Beautiful Marla. "I KNEW it! Liz and I talked it over last night! I thought for SURE I'd seen

139

you in a movie. And Liz said if I was right, then there must be some reason why you stopped acting and went into hiding!"

"You have a smart sister," said Clay.

"I know," said Marla.

Lee turned around. "Uncle Clay's a GOOD actor, too," he said. "We wish he'd act again."

"Who wants to see a scarred actor?" asked Clay. "I'm never going to act again!"

"That's so ROMANTIC!" said Marla.

"That's so stupid!" whispered Allie.

"Do your eyes hurt?" asked Delia.

Jinx remembered that yesterday she'd said maybe Clay wore sunglasses because his eyes hurt.

"You can act with your sunglasses on," said Jinx. "You'd be a mystery man."

"Yeah," said Drew. "You can really act.

140

Last night you had me fooled! Jinx and I were sure you were crazy."

"You can start acting this summer!" said Marla. "When you and Sonny and Lee come back to Ragged Island! We can put on a play in the town hall!"

Marla sent Sonny a dazzling smile.

"I think she has a play already in mind," murmured Allie.

"Yeah," said Liz. "She'll be the star. And he'll be her leading man."

"I'll think about it," said Clay. "Meanwhile I'm finally going to make those pancakes."

"Hooray!" said Delia.

Clay made great pancakes. Jinx ate four of them. One too many. He figured he'd better move around.

"Anyone want to go out?" he asked.

Only the adults stayed inside. Sonny took

The Beautiful Marla off to show her the puzzle garden. Delia wanted to go too. Sonny gave her a dollar not to.

"Looks like you'll be coming to Ragged Island every summer from now on," Drew said to Lee.

Lee grinned from ear to ear. "Looking forward to it," he said. "And I'm not likely to forget about the tides any time soon!"

Jinx looked around the grounds. Moody

Manor would probably be Roy's. That is, if the courts agreed he was Earl's son. Roy and Clay and the boys would probably do their own yard work. That meant no more job for Jinx! What about his new bike?

Jinx looked at the bushes he hoped he'd still be paid to cut. Under the biggest bush, next to the woodshed, he saw something yellow.

"What's that?" he said. "In the bushes near the woodshed?"

"Looks pretty big," said Liz.

"A boat motor?" guessed Allie

Jinx went to see. He reached into the bushes. He pulled on a metal tube. It must have been under the bush for a long time. It was hard to pull out.

"What is it?" asked Delia.

Jinx held out a rusty tricycle.

"My new bicycle!" said Jinx. "It just needs a new coat of paint!"

ABOUT THE AUTHOR

Michelle Dionetti loves mysteries, old wooden boxes, singing, subways, drawing, ancient Egypt, painting, and traveling anywhere she's never been before. She is athletic—that is, in her mind. She lives on the coast of Maine with her husband, who also writes. They have too many books—if there were such a thing as too many books. Her recent books include *Mice to The Rescue* and *Painting the Wind*.